THIS WALKER BOOK BELONGS TO:

_____

_____

_____

_____

For Andrew Nigel John – J.C.

For Ru – K.MᶜE.

First published 1998 by Walker Books Ltd
87 Vauxhall Walk, London SE11 5HJ

This edition published 1999

10 9 8 7 6 5 4 3

Text © 1998 June Crebbin
Illustrations © 1998 Katharine MᶜEwen

This book has been typeset in Myriad Tilt Bold.

Printed in Hong Kong

British Library Cataloguing in Publication Data
A catalogue record for this book is
available from the British Library

ISBN 0-7445-6947-8

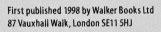

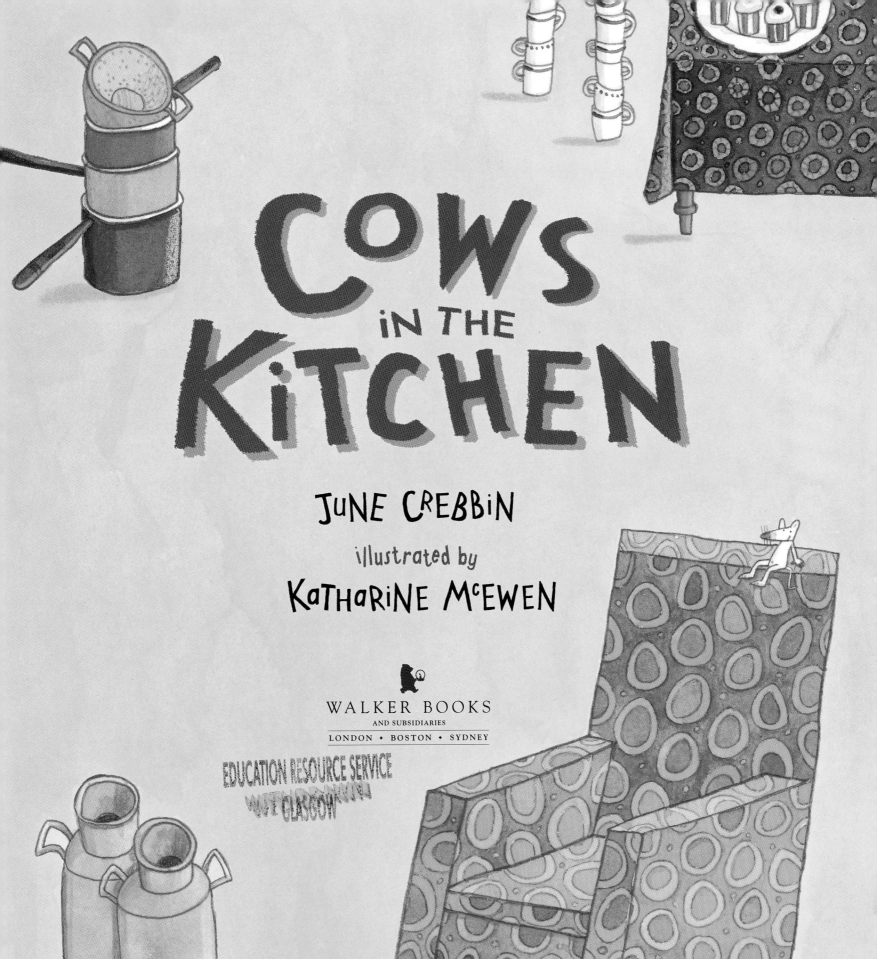

Cows
IN THE
Kitchen

JUNE CREBBIN

illustrated by
KATHARINE MᶜEWEN

WALKER BOOKS
AND SUBSIDIARIES
LONDON · BOSTON · SYDNEY

Cows in the kitchen, moo, moo, moo,
Cows in the kitchen, moo, moo, moo,

Cows in the kitchen, moo, moo, moo.
That's what we do, Tom Farmer!

Ducks on the dresser, quack, quack, quack,
Ducks on the dresser, quack, quack, quack,

Ducks on the dresser, quack, quack, quack.
That's what we do, Tom Farmer!

Pigs in the pantry, oink, oink, oink,
Pigs in the pantry, oink, oink, oink,

Pigs in the pantry, oink, oink, oink.
That's what we do, Tom Farmer!

Hens on the hatstand, cluck, cluck, cluck,
Hens on the hatstand, cluck, cluck, cluck,

Hens on the hatstand, cluck, cluck, cluck.
That's what we do, Tom Farmer!

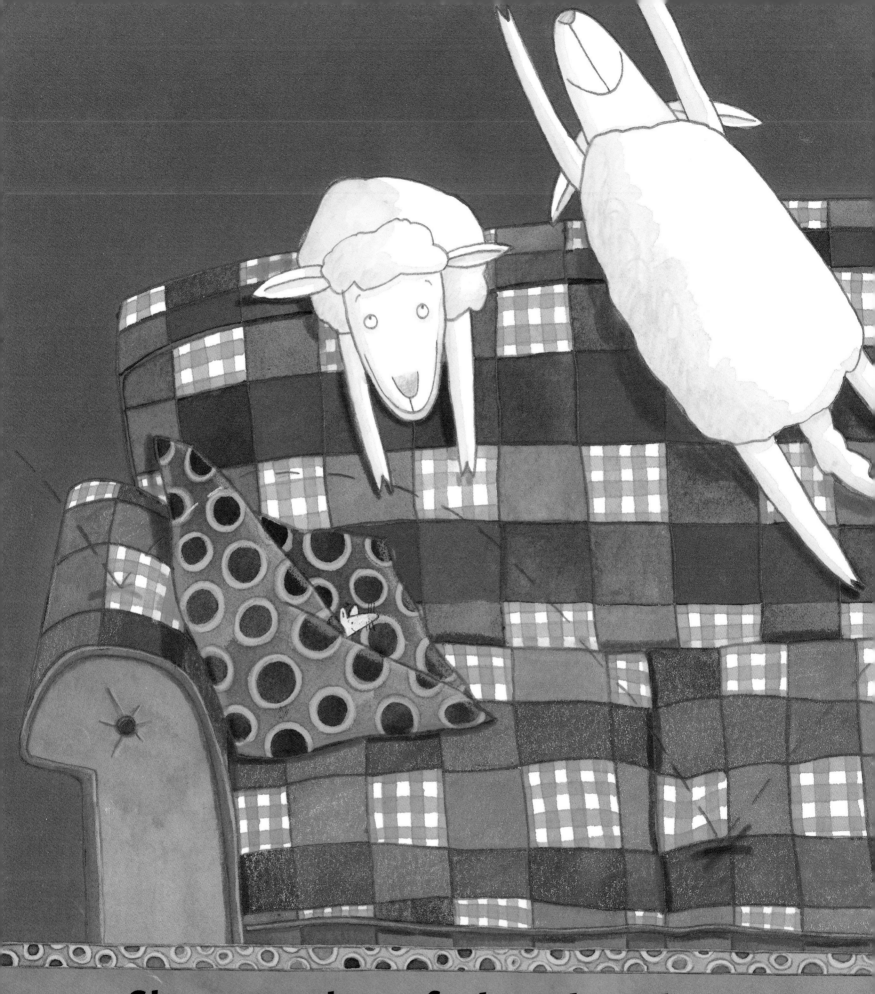

Sheep on the sofa, baa, baa, baa,
Sheep on the sofa, baa, baa, baa,

Sheep on the sofa, baa, baa, baa.
That's what we do, Tom Farmer!

Farmer in the haystack, zzz, zzz, zzz,
Farmer in the haystack, zzz, zzz, zzz,

Farmer in the haystack,

zzz, zzz, zzz . . .

TIME TO WAKE UP,

TOM FARMER!

Out of the farmhouse, shoo, shoo, shoo,
Out of the farmhouse, shoo, shoo, shoo,

Out of the farmhouse, shoo, shoo, shoo,
Shoo, shoo, shoo, shoo, shoo!

Farmer in the armchair, shhh, shhh, shhh,
Farmer in the armchair, shhh, shhh, shhh,

Farmer in the armchair, shhh, shhh, shhh,
Shhh, shhh, shhh, shhh, shhh.

Lift the latch, shhh, Shhh, Shhh.

Push the door, shhh, shhh, shhh.

Creep down the hall,

Shhh, Shhh, Shhh . . .

THAT'S WHAT WE DO,

TOM FARMER!

MORE WALKER PAPERBACKS
For You to Enjoy

FLY BY NIGHT
by June Crebbin/Stephen Lambert

All day long Blink, the young owl, sits on his branch, waiting patiently to take flight for the very first time. Will the moment ever arrive?

"A rich introduction to what a good story is all about – perfect for reading aloud and relishing the pictures." *Children's Books of the Year*

0-7445-3627-8   £4.99

THE TRAIN RIDE
by June Crebbin/Stephen Lambert

What could be finer than a train ride with Mum across country to the sea, where someone very special is waiting!

"There's lots to see, both on the bright red steam train and through its windows, with bold, strongly coloured illustrations of a hazy summer's day sweeping across the pages to draw you into the rhyme." *Practical Parenting*

0-7445-4701-6   £4.99

WE'RE GOING ON A BEAR HUNT
by Michael Rosen/Helen Oxenbury

We're going on a bear hunt.
We're going to catch a big one.
What a beautiful day!
We're not scared.

Winner of the Smarties Book Prize and
Highly Commended for the Kate Greenaway Medal.

"A dramatic and comic masterpiece…
Beautifully produced, written and illustrated, this is a classic."
The Independent on Sunday

0-7445-2323-0   £4.99